ANIMALIA

Hello, we must be going

'Owwww!'
Zoe rubbed her head and groaned.
The last thing she remembered
was swerving to avoid a kid on a
skateboard. Now her bike was
a total wreck.
Where was that boy?
She scanned the park, then spotted
him climbing the steps to the
Metro Library.

The kid had already reached the
information desk before she caught
up with him.
'Hey you! Speed racer!'
'Excuse me?' said the boy. He had
never heard anyone speak quite so
loudly in a library, ever.
'You bashed up my bike,' shouted
Zoe. Before she could say another
word her mobile phone began
to ring.

As the girl turned to take the call, Alex tiptoed off to the Adventure section. Unfortunately, Zoe was right behind him.

'He's on the move, but he's not getting away until he pays up!'

Alex led the pair into a reading room lined with old, leather-bound books. The room seemed strange. Zoe's phone went dead.

Suddenly the books parted, revealing a corridor of white light.

'I wonder where this leads?' gasped Alex.

'Hey, no slipping out the backdoor,' cried Zoe. 'You so owe me!'

The pair stumbled forward into a whole new dimension…

'Now what have you done?'
whispered Zoe.
They were still in the library,
but somehow the kids found
themselves face-to-face with
a lion and a rhinoceros.
There was stunned silence.
Then a deafening roar.
Alex and Zoe made a dash for
the exit, screaming all the way.

When they had gone, the rhinoceros frowned at the lion.
'You didn't give them a very friendly greeting.'
'I wanted to Reenie,' he explained, 'but you stepped
on my tail.'

Zoe and Alex fought to pull open the
library door, still shrieking with fright.
'Lion in the library!'
screeched Zoe.
Her voice suddenly trailed off.
'OK, who moved the city…?'

The world outside the library had become an exotic, jungle kingdom.
It was unlike anything they had ever seen before.
'Somebody's got a lot of explaining to do,' said Alex.
The pair ran down the steps and headed toward a restaurant.
It took several seconds before Alex realised it was full of animals.
Elephants in pinnies were serving zebras, foxes, even a tiger!
Everyone in the restaurant looked back at Alex and Zoe, then
screamed.
Alex and Zoe were already yelling their heads off…
and running.

'Argghh!'
Zoe and Alex scrambled through the jungle. Both were panting with tiredness, but taking a break wasn't an option right now.
Suddenly Zoe skidded to a halt at the edge of a steep bank. As she peered down at the wilderness below, Alex thudded into the back of her.
'WooooaahHHH!
The pair were sent tumbling over the edge. They fell through vines, only to crash and slide further and further downwards…

———◆———

The Elephant's Eaterie was in chaos.
'Ugliest things I ever did see!' gasped Zed Zebra.
'Maybe they were humans?' asked
Elni Elephant.
Melford Mouse twitched his nose.
'What are humans, Melba?'
'Mythical creatures,' said Melba Micely.
'Probably don't exist.'
Tyrannicus the tiger got up from his table.
'Whatever those things are, I don't trust them.
They look like monsters!'

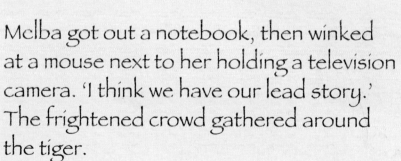

Melba got out a notebook, then winked
at a mouse next to her holding a television
camera. 'I think we have our lead story.'
The frightened crowd gathered around
the tiger.
'The very core of our society is crumbling,
my friends,' said Tyrannicus. 'Dark
clouds have blocked out the sun.
And now invaders. We need to
catch them!'

Reenie ran back into the library.
'Livingstone!' she cried. 'We're being invaded by monsters!
What shall we do?' The lion was staring at the Core, the huge rock at
the very heart of his kingdom. 'I'm a bit busy with this right now, Reenie.'
Up through the library skylight, dark clouds swirled overhead.
Things were not as they should be.
'I'm not sure what's wrong,' explained Livingstone. 'But we'd better
figure it out fast.'

'What is this place?' gasped Zoe. She and Alex were standing in the middle of a rainforest. The waterfalls, rocks and plants were beautiful – and seriously weird.

'It's unreal,' whispered Alex. 'I feel like I'm dreaming.'

Zoe gasped. 'That's it! When I wrecked my bike I must have been knocked out. Wake me up!'

Four pinches later and Zoe got the message. 'I'm up.'

Suddenly Alex pointed over Zoe's shoulder, gibbering wildly.

'Alli-geh-Alli-geh…'

An alligator rose up to its full height behind Zoe, flashing its impressive snappers

Zoe was totally unaware. She was far too busy pointing at the green gorilla that was looming up behind Alex.

9

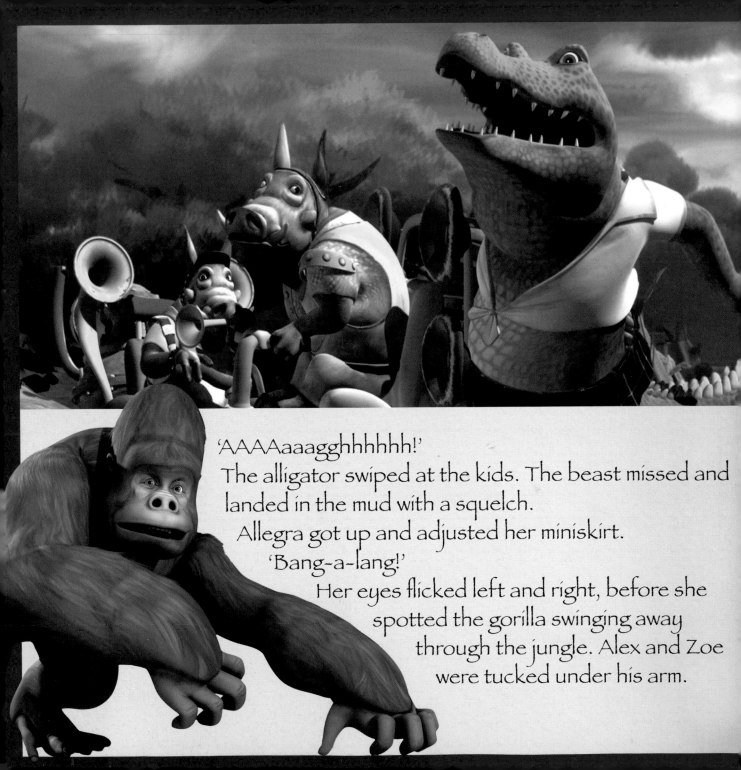

'AAAAaaagghhhhhh!'
The alligator swiped at the kids. The beast missed and landed in the mud with a squelch.

Allegra got up and adjusted her miniskirt.

'Bang-a-lang!'

Her eyes flicked left and right, before she spotted the gorilla swinging away through the jungle. Alex and Zoe were tucked under his arm.

Music blared out through the trees. Two horrible hogs on motorbikes came zooming into view.

'I just saw two new critters!' announced Allegra.

'SHE JUST ATE APPLE FRITTERS?' bellowed one of the hogs.

'Turn down that music Herry!' bawled Allegra.

Herry pushed a button on his boom box then grinned.

'That must be them monsters!'

'Everybody's talking about them!' added Horble.

Herry nodded. 'There's probably a reward for their capture.'

Allegra's black eyes glittered.

'Betcha whoever catches them will be the hero of Animalia.'

Allegra heaved herself on to the back of Horble's bike.

'Or heroine,' she corrected. 'Come on, they're getting away!'

The gorilla sat the kids on a tree branch, then tossed them
a couple of bananas.
'Tasty!' said Alex.
The gorilla grinned. 'So you can talk? Bonus!'
Alex's mouth fell open, spilling banana chunks everywhere.
'I love bananas!' beamed G'Bubu.
Zoe and Alex were so shocked to meet a talking ape that they toppled
backwards. G'Bubu leant over to watch the pair bump down through
the leaves. Finally they crashed through the roof of his treehouse.
'Well, they're definitely not birds.'

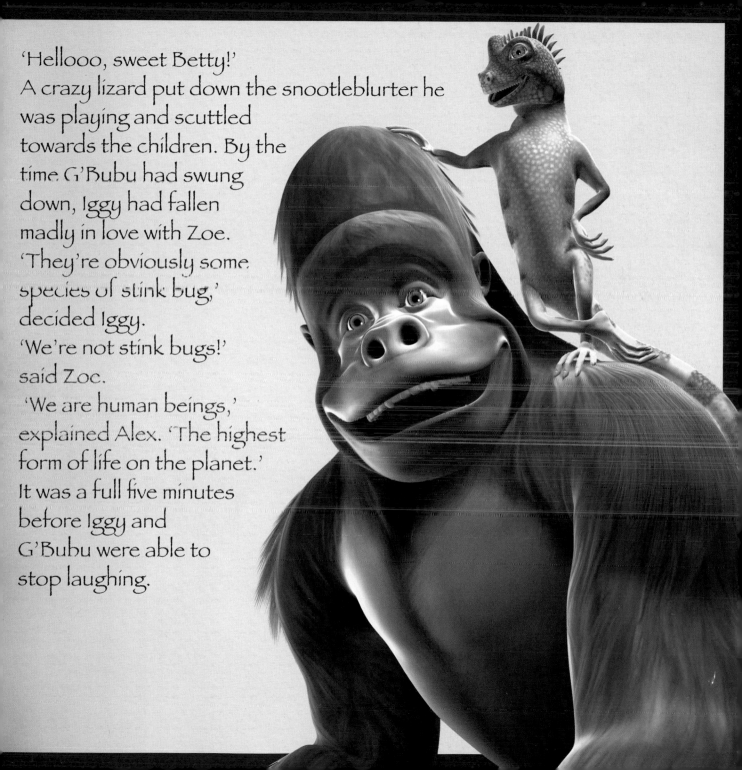

'Hellooo, sweet Betty!'
A crazy lizard put down the snootleblurter he
was playing and scuttled
towards the children. By the
time G'Bubu had swung
down, Iggy had fallen
madly in love with Zoe.
'They're obviously some
species of stink bug,'
decided Iggy.
'We're not stink bugs!'
said Zoe.
'We are human beings,'
explained Alex. 'The highest
form of life on the planet.'
It was a full five minutes
before Iggy and
G'Bubu were able to
stop laughing.

Alex and Zoe decided to leave the laughing animals. But before they could get anywhere, blue butterflies fluttered down in front of them.

'What's on their wings?' asked Alex.

G'Bubu grinned as a television picture formed on the butterflies' backs. 'That's the Animalia News!'

Two mice at a news desk began to read.

'Today, one month after the cracking of the Core, there's even more bad news.' said Melba Micely.

Melford Mouse leapt up from his seat. 'We're being invaded by monsters. Run for your lives!'

———◆✕◆———

Over at the library, Livingstone raised an eyebrow. 'I think there's something fishy about this monster story.'

Tyrannicus appeared on the fluttervision screen. 'It's time to buy Tyrannicus' home protection system. Easy payment plans available.'

'Hmm…' nodded Livingstone.

'That must be where the fishy smell is coming from.'

A cry from Reenie interrupted him.

'I've found it! The secret of the Core.'

The rhino had been searching the library's computer.

'What do you have?' asked Livingstone.

'It's not good,' frowned Reenie. 'Not good at all…'

'There they are! Get 'em!'
Allegra and the hogs burst out of
the bushes. The kids turned to
escape.
'Catch the invaders!'
Erno Elephant and Zed Zebra
had their exit route blocked.
Suddenly a force swept down
from nowhere and dragged the
children to safety – G'Bubu
and Iggy.

The runaways didn't stop 'til they
reached the top of Lookout Mountain.
From up there they could see all of
Animalia's beauty.
'Not too shabby,' said Zoe.
'You should see it when there are no
spooky clouds in the sky,' agreed Iggy.
'The clouds are new,' shrugged
G'Bubu. 'Just like you two.'
'Check this out,' cried Alex.
'It's some kind of plant.'

He was crouching by a small bush. Amongst its exotic flowers
was a blue seed.

'That's new too,' said G'Bubu.

As Alex picked up the glowing seed, it cracked open.

'Uber weird,' whispered Alex, gazing at the egg inside.

'Found 'em on Lookout Mountain!' called out a voice. Alex and Zoe
turned to see two zebras pointing at them from a low-flying zeppelin.
Down the mountainside, Allegra and her cronies were on their
trail again.

It was time for another quick getaway.

Alex and Zoe ran back through the jungle, towards the town square. Within minutes they were faced with an angry mob of Animalians.

'Step back,' squealed a voice. 'Those critters are mine!'

Allegra and the hogs pushed to the front. 'I chased 'em, so the reward belongs to me.'

'What reward?' asked Erno Elephant.

Allegra poked Horble Hog. 'You said there was a reward!'

'I said there was probably going to be a reward,' stumbled Horble.

Tyrannicus stepped past the angry alligator. 'These beasts are dangerous,' he warned. 'I'll take care of them.'

'Just because these stink bugs are new here, it doesn't mean they are monsters,' argued G'Bubu.

Tyrannicus turned to the crowd. 'They're monsters!'

'Just because they are goofy-looking, that doesn't make them monsters.'

The mob stepped forward. 'They're MONSTERS!'
G'Bubu had one last card to play. 'But they're
really funny! They claim to be the most
intelligent creatures on the planet.'
Tyrannicus looked carefully at Zoe and Alex,
then guffawed. The rest of the
Animalians were already on the floor,
helpless with laughter.

G'Bubu led Alex and Zoe up the steps to the Library.
'I'd like to introduce you to the ruler of Animalia.'
'Welcome,' smiled Livingstone. 'I suppose you have a few questions.'
'A few thousand,' nodded Alex.
Livingstone looked at Reenie. 'Let me see if I can explain.'
He pointed up to the glowing Core. Pictures of Animalia began to flutter
across its surface.
'Animalia has existed since the dawn of time,' began Livingstone.
'We have always lived in peace, thanks to a powerful skill that we share.
The power of words.'

Zoe glanced towards the library doors. G'Bubu was struggling to keep them shut. The crowd must have realised they had gone.

'A month ago the Core cracked,' said Livingstone. 'Some pieces of the Core flew out into the sky.'

The thumping on the doors got louder.

'Since then, we have fallen into darkness,' sighed Livingstone.

'I need you two to help restore the Core and save Animalia.'

'But how can we help?' asked Alex. 'We don't know where to start.'

Livingstone looked them both in the eye. 'We should start with what comes first.'

'Hmm…' mused Zoe. 'What comes first, the chicken or the egg?'

Alex punched the air.

'Egg-zactly!'

G'Bubu couldn't hold the doors any longer. Tyrannicus and his mob burst into the Library.

'Hand over the monsters Livingstone,' demanded the tiger.

Livingstone stood in front of Alex and Zoe. 'No monsters here.'

The crowd edged even closer.

'We may be new,' argued Alex. 'But that doesn't make us monsters.'

Tyrannicus shook his head. 'You don't fit in.'

'How do you know?' said Zoe.

'Because we've never seen anything like you,' snapped Allegra.

Alex reached behind his back, then pulled out the egg. The crowd fell back at once.

'Have you ever seen anything like this?' he cried. 'I don't know what's inside, but do you think it will fit in?'
Alex tossed the egg over to Zoe. She gently pushed it into the Core.
'It's a corespore!' cried Iggy.
There was a rush of energy as the Core bubbled and shone gold. A trail of light rocketed up to the sky. The clouds suddenly parted and disappeared.
'The sun is back!' cried Reenie.
'It's a bang-a-lang miracle!' squealed Allegra.
Everybody rushed outside to greet the sunshine.

'I don't know how to repay you,' smiled Livingstone. 'I didn't think the Core could be fixed so easily.'

'What do you mean?' asked Alex.

'Once there's a crack in the Core, things usually get worse.'

Then Alex's reply was drowned out by a rumbling noise. The Core cracked open, throwing pieces of rock in all directions.

'Looks like we've got more work to do,' said Livingstone.

Alex turned to Zoe. 'This could take a while.'

'I guess we're gonna be late for supper,' nodded Zoe.

Iggy gave G'Bubu a gorilla-sized hug. 'The stinkbugs are staying!'